# Detective Frankenstein

Alaya Johnson

illustrated by Yuko Ota

Graphic Universe™ • Minneapolis • New York

Story by Alaya Johnson

Pencils and inks by Yuko Ota

Coloring by Hi-Fi Design

Lettering by Marshall Dillon



Graphic Universe™
A division of Lerner Publishing Group, Inc.
241 First Avenue North
Minneapolis, MN 55401 U.S.A.

Website address: www.lernerbooks.com

Library of Congress Cataloging-in-Publication Data

Johnson, Alaya Dawn, 1982–
Detective Frankenstein / Alaya Johnson ; illustrated by Yuko Ota.
p. cm. — (Twisted journeys ; #17)
Summary: As a young servant in London in the late nineteenth century, thinking that fellow servant Eleanor has been murdered and the body snatched, the reader is asked to make choices to determine the outcome of the story.
ISBN: 978–0–8225–8942–6 (lib. bdg. : alk. paper)
1. Plot-your-own stories. 2. Graphic novels. [1. Graphic novels. 2. Murder—Fiction. 3. Body snatching—Fiction. 4. Mystery and detective stories. 5. Horror stories. 6. Plot-your-own stories.] I. Ota, Yuko, ill. II. Title.
PZ7.7.J64De 2011
741.5'973—dc22 2010028509

Manufactured in the United States of America
1 – DP – 12/31/10

ARE YOU READY FOR YOUR *Twisted Journeys®*? YOU ARE THE HERO OF THE BOOK YOU'RE ABOUT TO READ. YOUR JOURNEYS WILL TAKE YOU TO GRAVEYARDS AND CREEPY MANSIONS IN 1890s LONDON, WHERE GRAVE ROBBERS ARE HARD AT WORK. AND EVERY STORY STARS ***YOU!***

EACH PAGE TELLS WHAT HAPPENS AS ***YOU*** HELP A FAMOUS DETECTIVE SOLVE THE MYSTERIES LEFT BEHIND BY THE LATE DOCTOR VICTOR FRANKENSTEIN. ***YOUR*** WORDS AND THOUGHTS ARE SHOWN IN THE ***YELLOW BALLOONS.*** AND ***YOU*** GET TO DECIDE WHAT HAPPENS NEXT. JUST FOLLOW THE NOTE AT THE BOTTOM OF EACH PAGE UNTIL YOU REACH A *Twisted Journeys®* PAGE. THEN MAKE THE CHOICE ***YOU*** LIKE BEST.

BUT BE CAREFUL... THE WRONG CHOICE COULD MAKE A MONSTER OUT OF YOU!

The knock comes long after sunset, when even old Silas the cook has fallen asleep by the fire. Mice squeak and skitter away as you stand up. Your friend Eleanor, the scullery maid, hasn't come back home yet. You know cautious Eleanor would never rap on the servant's door so loudly. Not when your miserly employer, Master Igor, would send you both back to the orphanage if he woke. You warned her not to go out so late. You were worried about *resurrection men*—the thieves who steal fresh bodies for men of science like Master Igor to experiment on. Eleanor just laughed at your worry.

And now . . .

You open the door. It's a copper, with his blue uniform and billy club. Your heart sinks.

"Does a young lady with red hair work here?" he asks.

You find your voice. "Eleanor! What's . . ."

The constable puts a meaty hand on your shoulder. "I'm so sorry," he says. "We found her in an alley an hour ago."

You're dazed as you hear the copper's next dreadful word:

"Murder."



GO ON TO THE NEXT PAGE.

GO ON TO THE NEXT PAGE.

GO ON TO THE NEXT PAGE.

"Resurrection men took her!" you say to the copper Bushwick. The one called Clive has turned pale.

"Clive," says Bushwick. "Who was that man you were just speaking to?"

"A murder witness, that's all," says Clive. "I'm sure he had nothing to do with this."

"Is even Scotland Yard not safe from the resurrection men?" says Bushwick.

The thought of those ruffians selling bodies for experiments makes you furious. But what can you do?

"Sorry," Bushwick says to you. "We'll tell you if we find anything."

Feeling numb, you walk outside. You want to find the thief, but you don't even know where to begin.

A tall man walks up behind you. "Some trouble?" he asks.

"Resurrection men," you say.

The man takes a long puff on his pipe. "Ah. Perhaps I can help you with that."

You look up, and then gasp. It's Lance Crosdale himself!

He chuckles at your expression. "Well? I'm a busy man. Do you want my help or not?"

GO ON TO THE NEXT PAGE.

# WILL YOU . . .

. . . accept the help of your hero to find Eleanor?
TURN TO PAGE 88.

. . . hurry back home to tell Master Igor what happened?
TURN TO PAGE 18.

"I have to sleep, sir," you say. "Maybe in the morning."

Igor slumps back in his chair. He waves you off and mutters to himself. "Frankenstein abandoned me. And now you will too. No good, the lot of you."

You practically sprint out the door. You can hardly wait for this day to end.

But when you try to sleep that night, your dreams are weird and twisted. Once, you think you hear Eleanor begging for your help. In the morning, you're still exhausted.

"I have to leave," you say to yourself. And it's true. You can't bear to be at Master Igor's anymore. Not after all that's happened. You take some food from the kitchen and what meager items belong to you. You're gone before the sun has fully risen.

You're not sure what you will do, but the world seems full of opportunities with Master Igor's dark house at your back.

THE END

WE FOUND OUT TWO MONTHS AGO.
HAS HE ALWAYS BEEN... A MONSTER?
IGOR KILLED HIM A YEAR AGO. CROSDALE HAD LEARNED TOO MUCH ABOUT HIS DEALINGS WITH RESURRECTION MEN.
BUT... CROSDALE IS STILL ALIVE!
THAT *THING* ISN'T THE CROSDALE YOU KNOW.
IT'S A MONSTER. AND I OWE IT TO MY FRIEND TO PUT HIM OUT OF HIS MISERY.
YOUR VOICE STICKS IN YOUR THROAT. YOU CAN'T BELIEVE THAT ALL THIS TIME YOU TRUSTED A MONSTER.
THIS ENDS HERE, CROSDALE.
BANG
HE LOOKS... PEACEFUL.
I'LL TAKE YOU HOME.
NO. NOT BACK THERE.
YOU NEVER FORGET THE MOMENT YOU LOST YOUR HERO. YOU BECOME A DETECTIVE AND DEDICATE YOURSELF TO STOPPING MASTER IGOR AND THE RESURRECTION MEN.
THE END

"Fine," you say to Travers. "I'm willing to do anything."

Travers's smile grows wider. "A runaway, are you?"

You shrug. "Does it matter?"

Travers shakes his head. "Not at all. Meet me here this evening. Work like ours doesn't get started until the sun goes down."

At dusk, you return to the inn. Now Travers is with two other resurrection men. They take you to Kensal Green, the famous old cemetery. You climb the wall with your shovels and bags. Then Travers sets you to work. The job is strangely peaceful. You don't mind the exercise. It makes it easier to forget about Eleanor and Master Igor. Months pass, then years. You become good at your job. You make a nice living selling the bodies you dig up to scientists and others for medical research.

You make a point to never sell to Master Igor, though. You always wondered what he did with the bodies, but you knew it couldn't be good.

**THE END**

"I don't think so, Eleanor," you say. "Let's stay here and see what the earl has to say."

Eleanor sighs, but she agrees.

Your bed is more luxurious than anything you could have imagined. The pillows are stuffed with feathers, and a servant puts a hot brick beneath the covers to warm your feet. In the morning, you dress and meet the earl in his library.

"My dears! Goodness, has anyone ever told you how much you resemble each other? I wonder . . . but here, have some breakfast."

You can hardly believe the food he offers you: eggs, bacon, sausage, kidneys, and thick porridge.

"I've never eaten so fine in my life!" you say.

"Well, if you two do as I ask, you will always eat like this."

Eleanor isn't as excited about the food. "And what do you want?" she asks.

Bridgeport touches his gold pocket watch. "I want you to sneak into Ichabod Igor's home and find where he has hidden Doctor Frankenstein's diary."

"Why his diary?" you ask.

"Once I expose the secrets inside, Eleanor will regain her rightful inheritance."



GO ON TO THE NEXT PAGE.

BRIDGEPORT! YOU HAVEN'T FOUND...
I THOUGHT I'D SEE HOW YOUR WORK WAS PROGRESSING, DOCTOR.
PREPARE M ROOMS, YO TWO.
NO ONE EVER PAYS SERVAN MUCH ATTENTION. YOU AND ELEANOR CAN EASILY EXPLO THE HOUSE NOW.
IT'S FUNNY...
WE'VE LIVED HERE ALMOST ALL OUR LIVES, AND YET...
WHERE DO WE START TO LOOK?
WHAT'S THAT?
LOOKS LIKE WE FOUND SOMETHING.
BUT *WHAT* DID YOU FIND?

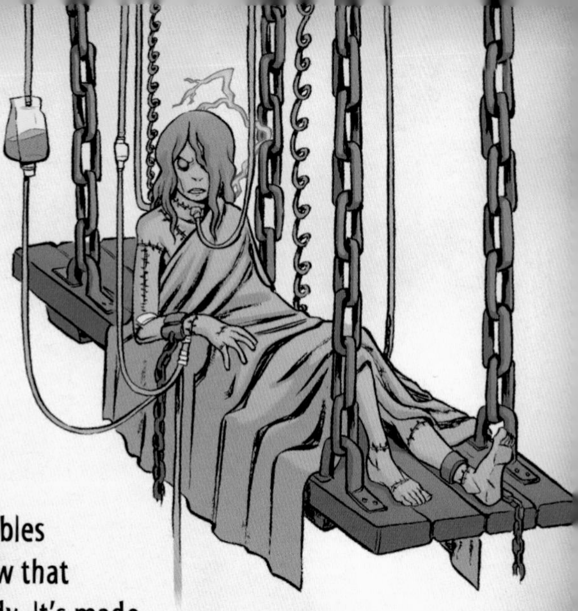

You gasp. "This must be . . ."

"His secret lab," Eleanor whispers. "Where he *creates* the monsters."

On the table near the wall, a body is connected to a ceiling contraption with cables and wires. You know that it isn't a normal body. It's made from the bits and pieces of other people, stolen from graveyards by resurrection men.

"Come on," Eleanor says. She walks ahead, but her shoulders tremble. She's frightened too. "We need to find Frankenstein's diary."

"What about that . . . *thing*?"

She gulps. "It's not alive."

You start to look for the diary. But neither of you find it. Then, from behind, you hear a gurgle. Something rattles.

"Eleanor," you say, "is that you?"

"I'm right here," she says, beside you.

Slowly, you both turn around. The creature on the table is moving . . .



GO ON TO THE NEXT PAGE.

The monster lets out another gurgle.

WILL YOU . . .

. . . run away? You don't want to be monster dinner.
TURN TO PAGE 41.

. . . hide behind a chest of drawers?
TURN TO PAGE 36.

GO ON TO THE NEXT PAGE.

"Officer Clive is planning something terrible," you whisper. "You have to get away!"

"I suspected something of the sort. I'll lead us someplace safer."

You tell Crosdale of the conversation you overheard, while you duck through alleys and lamplit streets. You don't recognize anything until you see the gates of Kensal Green, a high-class cemetery in East London. All sorts of famous people are buried here—even the infamous Doctor Frankenstein. The gates are closed, but Detective Crosdale leads you to an ivy-covered section of the wall. He scrambles over the top.

"Hurry!" he says, when you hesitate.

You don't like graveyards, but you're not safe out in the open. You take Detective Crosdale's hand and climb over the wall. The graveyard is eerie, yet peaceful. You have entered the domain of the dead. The world the resurrection men steal from and people like Master Igor use for profit.

You shudder.

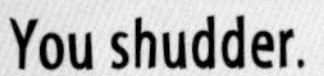

TURN TO PAGE 103.

You wish the walk home could last forever. Then you would never have to go back to your boring life as a servant for Master Igor. You almost wish you had accepted Detective Crosdale's offer. But you know how hard it is to find good work in this city. You can't risk it. When you arrive home, you are surprised to see the lamps still lit in Master Igor's quarters. You knock on his door.

"Oh, it's you," Master Igor says. "Come in, come in. I have need of company tonight."

Something is strange about Master Igor. You take a few steps closer and understand. He's been drinking! Master Igor pours himself a glass of brandy and nods in your direction.

"To knowledge!" he says. "Which I have finally disposed of today."

"Y-you have?" you say. You don't know what to think. You've never seen Master Igor behave quite like this before.

"All I ever wanted was knowledge and power. Did I ever tell you how I came to learn the sciences?"

GO ON TO THE NEXT PAGE.

I WAS BORN IN SWITZERLAND. I NEVER KNEW MY PARENTS. JUST THE ORPHANAGE. THE OTHER CHILDREN TREATED ME CRUELLY.

I UNDERSTOOD THAT I COULD USE SCIENCE TO GAIN MASTERY OVER THEM. I BECAME DETERMINED TO PROVE MYSELF TO THE WORLD.

I RECEIVED A FELLOWSHIP TO STUDY SCIENCE AT THE UNIVERSITY. FOR A TIME, ALL WAS WELL...

SNIVELING DOLT!
MOCK US IN CLASS, WILL YOU?
I WAS LEFT FOR DEAD IN AN ALLEY...I HAD NO STRENGTH TO RETURN TO MY STUDIES.

ONLY DOCTOR FRANKENSTEIN PITIED ME. ONLY HE UNDERSTOOD MY NEED FOR KNOWLEDGE.
ONLY HE KNEW WHAT IT WAS LIKE TO FEEL POWERLESS. AND THEN HE GAVE ME THE ULTIMATE POWER...

WOULD YOU LIKE TO SEE THE TRUE FACE OF POWER?

GO ON TO THE NEXT PAGE.

Master Igor is acting very creepy. Do you really want to encourage him?

# WILL YOU . . .

. . . agree? You're a little curious.
TURN TO PAGE 43.

. . . tell him you're tired and back out slowly? You don't trust Master Igor in this mood.
TURN TO PAGE 9.

Is that her head you see disappearing down the left-hand street? Not many people are out this late, but the streetlamps are so dim, it's hard to see clearly. You sprint forward, but you don't see her. Up ahead, someone slams a door shut. A baby cries in the night. Something is wrong here, but what? You hear heavy footsteps behind you.

"Eleanor," you whisper. "Is that you?"

But the figure behind you is much too large to be your friend. In fact, it seems to be *glowing* as it shambles toward you.

"Go . . . away . . ." it groans. "Away . . ."

The thing steps into the light. It's a monster! There are great stitches down his neck, and his skin glows.

You stumble backward, but not quickly enough. The monster puts his hands on your shoulders. You feel something sizzle and your hair stands on end, and that's the last you know.

***THE END***

You climb over the gate, right behind Eleanor.

"I told you to leave!"

You hand her the bag from the morgue. "You forgot this."

She has tears in her eyes when she opens the watch. "Oh, thank you! I thought that I had lost it forever when they kidnapped me."

"But who kidnapped you?"

She frowns. "I don't know. But I overheard them speak, and I think it was Master Igor who ordered it. He wanted everyone to think I was dead."

Master Igor? Your jaw drops. "Why would Master Igor do such a thing?"

"I don't know. But I wonder . . . back at the orphanage the nuns always hinted I might be in danger . . ."

You and Eleanor grew up in the same orphanage. And you have strange memories too. But you don't have a chance to ask any other questions. On the street, someone screams. You hear a roar . . .



GO ON TO THE NEXT PAGE.

GO ON TO THE NEXT PAGE.

That monster looks incredibly dangerous, and you hate the resurrection men anyway. Do you really want to risk yourself to save him?

## WILL YOU . . .

. . . hide?
TURN TO PAGE 28.

. . . try to stop the monster?
TURN TO PAGE 57.

"Officer!" you call. The man looks up at you. He smells of liquor. "Someone in that alley stole something from us!"

The police officer burps. Then he looks you up and down. Suddenly, you're embarrassed about your threadbare servant's clothing.

"Stole from *you*?" he says. "You two don't look like you have half a farthing between you."

"You're the police!" Eleanor says. "You have to help us!"

She grabs him by the elbow. But the officer shakes her off.

"We'll just be going now," you say.

"How now. I think you two urchins need to be taught your place."

Before you know it, other police have surrounded you. The two of you are handcuffed and tossed into jail. You try begging anyone for help, but they don't believe you. In the morning, you're released, but it's too late for the clues. Earl Bridgeport refuses to see you. Detective Crosdale vanishes, and he's never heard from again.

***THE END***

Ichabod Igor was my apprentice. A genius. He understood all my work. He believed in my mission of restoring life to the dead.
But he was unscrupulous. He wanted to use my invention for money and fame. And his friend, the earl, wanted to use it for politics.
Igor poisoned my wine.
SOMEONE, FETCH THE DOCTOR!
Eleanor, your maid knew Igor would kill you next...

"I'll need to know more," you tell Travers, warily. He tells you all about how the resurrection men choose graves. How they hide the bodies. Who buys them. Scientists and universities, mostly, for research and training medical students. But there's the occasional mystery customer, like Master Igor. You promise to meet Travers that night, but as soon as you leave, you go straight to Scotland Yard.

"I need to speak with Detective Crosdale," you tell the officer out front.

"You again?" Crosdale says when he meets you in the lobby. "You refused my help, and I have no time now. What do you want?"

You're disappointed at his coldness. But even so, you tell him what you've learned.

Crosdale taps his foot. "Resurrection men? Why, they're a dime a dozen. This has nothing to do with any important case."

Crosdale hurries off. You're about to go when someone coughs behind you.

It's the copper who first told you of Eleanor's death! "If you'd like to go after resurrection men," he says, "I'll help you."

TURN TO PAGE 77.

You huddle with Eleanor behind some ivy. Maybe the monster hasn't noticed you. The resurrection man screams again. Eleanor looks anxiously at the door.

"I don't think this is right," she whispers. "We can't just leave him there."

"We have to," you say. "Otherwise, we might get hurt too." You try to whisper as softly as possible, but the monster hears you anyway.

"Where is she?" it roars. The monster tears the ivy from the wall. You stare at it in terror. The ripped suit is frighteningly familiar. And the cracked pipe between its lips . . .

"You tell me where she is!" the monster—no—*Detective Crosdale* roars.

"Get away, Eleanor!" That's all you have time to shout before the monster grabs you by the throat. Then everything goes black.

***THE END***

Travers is a resurrection man!

# WILL YOU . . .

. . . take the job? Maybe it isn't so bad as it sounds.
TURN TO PAGE 11.

. . . ask as many questions as you can about the job and then give the information to Detective Crosdale? Maybe that way you can get back in his good graces.
TURN TO PAGE 27.

I'M NOT SO SURE ABOUT THIS...

YOU! YOU SHOULD BE...
DEAD? SORRY TO DISAPPOINT YOU.

AND IT TURNS OUT THAT WE'RE BOTH FRANKENSTEIN'S HEIRS.

B-BUT...
WE WANT YOU TO HELP CROSDALE. YOU'RE THE ONLY ONE WHO CAN.

WHY SHOULD I?

HE'LL HELP IF WE PROMISE TO DENY EVERYTHING CHARLIE PUTS IN THE PAPER. THAT MEANS GIVING UP OUR INHERITANCE, BUT...

TURN TO PAGE 83.

"No," you say to Eleanor. "How can we trust her? She's a monster. We should help Bridgeport."

Eleanor hesitates. "Well . . . maybe you're right."

So you hide when Master Igor enters the room. "Nothing here . . ." he mutters.

You both breathe a sigh of relief when he leaves. You also leave a few minutes later. Unfortunately, the hallway isn't empty.

"I thought it might be you two," says a voice from behind you.

You whirl around, terrified that Master Igor has found you. But it's just the earl.

"Oh!" Eleanor says. "You scared us."

"Be more careful. Igor nearly caught you here. Have you found the diary?"

"Not yet," you admit.

Bridgeport frowns. "You might try his study in the tower but hurry. Igor will be suspicious if we stay longer than a day. Do whatever you need to—but don't get caught."

GO ON TO THE NEXT PAGE.

Eleanor squares her shoulders. "Only one way to know where to find the diary. We have to investigate Igor."

"How?" you ask.

She grins. "By following him, of course."

You cover your heads with your hoods and creep down the hallways until you find Master Igor, pacing in his bedroom.

"What is that Bridgeport scheming?" Master Igor mutters, running his hands over his bald head. "Maybe I should move the diary. No, no . . . there's no way he could find it. Not *there*."

You and Eleanor share a wide-eyed look. Igor has the diary, but where has he hidden it?

"No," Igor repeats. "Even Crosdale hasn't thought to look there."

He reaches into his pocket and pulls out a long brass key. He presses it briefly to his lips. "Not even you could find it, Crosdale. The Green is the last place you'll ever look."

"That could be the key to his study," you whisper to Eleanor.

She nods. "But are you sure the diary is there? What did he mean by 'the green'?"

The word rings a bell. "Could he mean . . . Kensal Green? The graveyard?"



GO ON TO THE NEXT PAGE.

"Where should we look?" Eleanor asks. "The study or the graveyard?"

# WILL YOU . . .

. . . go to the study? Igor could be hiding something there.
TURN TO PAGE 67.

. . . waste no time and head directly to Kensal Green?
TURN TO PAGE 85.

"Let's give the diary to Crosdale," you say. "I trust him. And he knows more about this than we do."

"But isn't he still in Earl Bridgeport's dungeon?" she asks.

Suddenly the urchin smiles. "Not anymore," he says. "I heard he escaped. But I'll help you find him."

"You're not a beggar, are you?" Eleanor says, suspiciously. "What are you doing here?"

The boy sighs. "I work for the paper. Charlie Anders, at your service. My sources tell me there's a bounty on Crosdale's head. Do you want my help to find him?"

Neither of you trusts him, but you agree anyway. In the alley where the boy first stole the photographs, Charlie picks up a scrap of blue cloth from a detective's uniform. "Could Crosdale have come after us?" you say.

He sniffs the cloth, and you see a rust-colored stain. "It looks like he's run afoul of someone. Let's ask in the tavern," Charlie says. "Stick close to me. It's dangerous in there."

Charlie can't be much older than you, but you believe him.

TURN TO PAGE 51.

TWISTED JOURNEYS®

Crosdale is acting strange. If he doesn't care about resurrection men, why take you to the graveyard?

# WILL YOU . . .

. . . stay and see what else you can do to help him?
TURN TO PAGE 106.

. . . leave quickly, before he gets you into trouble?
TURN TO PAGE 69.

OH, PLEASE HELP ME. WHAT DID I DO TO DESERVE THIS FATE?
IS THAT...THE MONSTER?
OH, LANCE, MY LOVE. WHERE ARE YOU?
SHE DOESN'T SEEM DANGEROUS.
WHO ARE YOU?
I AM...I **WAS** ISABEL CRANMER.
I SAW YOUR HEADSTONE!

YES. ICHABOD IGOR KILLED ME AND THEN USED HIS EVIL TECHNIQUES TO REANIMATE ME IN THIS MONSTROUS HALF-LIFE.
BUT WHY?
LANCE AND I WERE ENGAGED TO BE MARRIED. BUT LANCE HAD LEARNED THE TRUTH ABOUT IGOR. SO IGOR KILLED AND REANIMATED ME TO PUNISH MY LOVE.

Just then, you hear a sound in the hallway behind the secret door.

"What's that?" a man calls from the hallway. You can't quite place the voice.

Eleanor moves to free Isabel, but the monster stops her. "No," she whispers, "you must help Lance. He's been captured. I overheard that horrible earl say so."

"Earl Bridgeport?" you ask.

She nods. "Yes. He's been working with Igor for some time now."

The door begins to open. "Hurry!" she whispers. "Please help him!"

You look at Eleanor. How are you supposed to escape with Igor at the door?

"Over here," Eleanor says, gesturing to the window.

You look out. That ledge looks steep! And there's only a little bit of ivy to help you down.

"That doesn't look safe . . ." you say.

Eleanor grins. "Afraid?"

GO ON TO THE NEXT PAGE.

That drop is really scary.

## WILL YOU . . .

. . . trust Isabel and go to find Detective Crosdale? You want to help him if he's in trouble.
TURN TO PAGE 62.

. . . convince Eleanor to keep looking for the diary and help Earl Bridgeport?
TURN TO PAGE 31.

You chase after the departing thieves, and Eleanor follows you. They're fast, but you're faster. You grab the smaller one.

"Wait, stop!" says the thief. You look down and realize that the thief is a kid, a little younger than you.

Eleanor is behind you. "They're just children," she says. "Let her go."

Reluctantly, you release your grip on the girl. The other one—an older boy—hasn't run away. He eyes you warily. In his right hand, he holds what looks like a bunch of papers.

"If you give that back," Eleanor says, "I'll give you two farthings."

The boy considers it. "There's a hidden message in these. For half a crown, I'll give it back and help you find what it leads to."

"He must mean the clues!" Eleanor says.

"Well? Do you want my help?" asks the boy.

GO ON TO THE NEXT PAGE.

Maybe you and Eleanor can solve the clues alone.

# WILL YOU . . .

. . . agree to get help from the urchin?
TURN TO PAGE 45.

. . . take the papers from the urchin and go on your own way?
TURN TO PAGE 109.

You push Eleanor ahead of you. "We have to leave!"

"We still haven't found the diary!"

"We can't do that if we're monster food!"

Eleanor seems to agree with this, and she scrambles ahead. Behind you, the monster has started to scream. Now you can hear the faint sounds of lightning crashing outside. Is that why the monster awoke now? You push the lever for the secret door, but it's stuck. You hit it again. The door starts to open. You look at it in relief, until you realize that someone is coming through the other side. Too late, you recognize Master Igor.

"You!" he says, when he enters the room. "He swore he finished you off!"

"You can't hurt me," Eleanor says. "I know who I am now."

Master Igor laughs cruelly. "We'll see about that."

GO ON TO THE NEXT PAGE.

The police arrive soon after.

"I found these two trespassing on my property and stealing the silver," Master Igor says. You appeal to Earl Bridgeport for help, but he just apologizes to Igor, saying he didn't realize he had hired two "dirty thieves."

"It will be all right," Eleanor says, as the coppers arrest you both and toss you in jail. "We'll find a way out of this."

But you two are just servants, and the judge doesn't believe in mercy for the lower classes. You and Eleanor are sentenced to five years of hard labor.

Three years into your sentence, Master Igor dies in a mysterious fall down his staircase. There are stories of a lightning storm the night of his accident, and some say they saw two hulking figures climbing over the garden wall. You and Eleanor are released on good behavior soon after.

As you walk down the London streets for the first time in three years, you wonder what you will do with your lives.

"I thought I might write a book," you say.

"No one will believe you," Eleanor says.

You smile. "I'll pretend it's just a story."

**THE END**

GO ON TO THE NEXT PAGE.

You can hardly believe your eyes. Those old stories of Doctor Frankenstein and his monsters are true!

## WILL YOU . . .

. . . become Master Igor's apprentice? You may never have this kind of opportunity again.
TURN TO PAGE 54.

. . . refuse to participate in these horrors?
TURN TO PAGE 71.

"We could use the help," you say. The urchin boy grins and happily pockets your money.

"Right, then," he says. He spreads out the papers. They're actually photographs! You see things that make you wince: bodies on metal gurneys, hooked up to long wires. A brain in a jar and other disembodied organs.

"What is all this?" Eleanor whispers. "And why does it look so familiar?"

Suddenly, you understand. "The brickwork of the wall," you point out. "Doesn't it look just like Master Igor's?"

"His experiments?" she asks.

You nod. And if Detective Crosdale truly is one of his monsters, then he must have seen all of these things.

The urchin looks thoughtful. "They always did say that Igor did evil things in his place." He turns over one of the photographs, and you see something scribbled in the corner. It's a name: Priscilla Warner.

"But who is that?" you ask.

The urchin stands. "Come, I'll take you."

GO ON TO THE NEXT PAGE.

PRISCILLA, I'VE BROUGHT TWO PEOPLE TO SEE YOU. THEY WANT TO KNOW ABOUT OLD MASTER IGOR.
MASTER IGOR? THAT VILLAIN?
I SERVED AS THE HANDMAID FOR YOUNG MRS. FRANKENSTEIN, WHEN THEY FIRST MOVED TO LONDON. AH, SHE WAS A BEAUTIFUL LASS!
BUT THAT HORRIBLE MASTER IGOR! HE POISONED THEIR FIRST CHILD, THOUGH WE DIDN'T KNOW IT AT THE TIME...
I TOOK THE SECOND CHILD TO AN ORPHANAGE, FEARING FOR ITS SAFETY.
WAAAAAAAAA
PLEASE, TAKE GOOD CARE OF THE BABE. NO ONE CAN EVER KNOW WHAT I'VE DONE!
AND AFTER DOCTOR FRANKENSTEIN DIED, I KNEW I HAD TO HIDE DEAR ELEANOR, AS WELL. BUT COULD IT BE...

Office Bushwick is still in the morgue. He looks startled when you come inside. "Officer Clive said he wants to speak with you," you say.

Officer Bushwick steps closer to you. "Where's Clive?"

You take a deep breath. "He says out back. The meeting place."

You pretend to leave but hide around a corner so he can't see you. Soon enough, he starts striding down the dark hallway you remember from before. You follow, moving so fast that you don't notice the broom in your path until it's too late. You fall down, and Bushwick turns around.

"I knew it!" he says. "Nosy little kid. Can't have you ruining our plans."

You struggle, but the copper picks you up and locks you in the storage closet. You yell, but no one hears you. In the morning, the commissioner lets you out. His sad face warns you before he speaks the awful truth.

Detective Crosdale is dead. Murdered in the night.

***THE END***

"Fine," you say to her. "Go ahead."

Eleanor looks at you suspiciously. Then she shrugs and climbs the cemetery wall. You wait until she's over before scrambling up behind her. You can't let her do this on her own.

As soon as you hop over the wall, you spot her red hair farther down the street. You hurry to follow her. It's easy on the mostly deserted streets near Kensal Green, but then she walks into a more crowded neighborhood. You can't get too close, because then she might notice you. But if you get too far away . . .

Somebody steps on your foot. You're distracted for a moment too long. When you look back up, you can't find Eleanor anywhere.

You run ahead, hoping to find her again. The street ends, branching right and left.

GO ON TO THE NEXT PAGE.

Eleanor could only have gone one of two ways. But you'd better guess correctly, or you might never find her.

# WILL YOU . . .

. . . turn left?
TURN TO PAGE 21.

. . . turn right?
TURN TO PAGE 95.

"Let's keep going," you whisper to Eleanor. You and Eleanor try to be extra careful as you follow Igor to the base of his tower. Then Master Igor whirls around. There's something in his hands. Not a key but a small silver gun!

"Aha!" Igor says, grinning madly. "I knew Bridgeport would double-cross me. He should have hired quieter spies."

"Don't shoot!" Eleanor says.

Igor turns pale with shock. "*You!* I thought . . . I say . . ."

"You hired those men to kill me, didn't you?"

Igor sneers. "They were supposed to get you both, in fact. So why would Bridgeport keep you alive now?"

"Us both?" you say. "But Eleanor is Frankenstein's heir . . ."

Igor laughs. "But with her out of the way, there would still be another child for the inheritance. We were only safe with you *both* gone."

You and Eleanor turn to each other.

"We're . . ." Eleanor starts.

"Siblings?" you finish.

Igor points the gun at her. "Not for long."

"Eleanor!" you shout, "run!"

You sprint at Igor. You only have time to hear Eleanor's footsteps scrambling away before the gun goes off, loud in your ears.

As the world fades to black, you can only hope Eleanor got away.

THE END

INSIDE THE TAVERN, YOU DISCOVER...
LET HIM GO!
HE'S SAFER TO ME DEAD, IF HE WON'T AGREE TO STOP HIS INVESTIGATIONS. IT'S HURTING BUSINESS.

ELEANOR, WATCH OUT!

HE'S GOT A GUN, STAY BACK!

BANG!!

STOP!
THIS IS A FRONT-PAGE STORY...

GO ON TO THE NEXT PAGE.

Charlie's run off with the memoirs! But Crosdale is hurt.

# WILL YOU . . .

. . . stay and help Crosdale?
TURN TO PAGE 91.

. . . chase after Charlie?
TURN TO PAGE 94.

"All right," you say. You open the door and check the hallway. There's no one outside. You and Eleanor creep through the house, hiding whenever a servant comes near.

"We need something to prove our story," Eleanor whispers as you near the exit.

You remember the drawing of Doctor Frankenstein and his child that Igor showed you when he told you who your parents were. "Follow me!" you say.

You open the secret door to his workroom. The motionless monsters don't scare you anymore, but Eleanor covers her mouth to hide a shriek of surprise.

"Over here," you say. You pull a book from a dusty pile. This is where Master Igor kept the picture. You show it to Eleanor. Her hands tremble as she looks at the image of her parents.

"They seem so happy . . ." she whispers.

Suddenly, you're sure you made the right decision.

A week later, a judge forces Master Igor to give his grand house and all his money to Doctor Frankenstein's rightful heirs. And you and Eleanor share everything.

You take a deep breath. "Yes," you say. What Master Igor just did with those bodies was incredible, even if a small part of you also finds it horrifying. Master Igor smiles.

"Excellent," he says.

For the next week, you are busy learning all Master Igor's secrets. There are many horrors in his labs. There are people he has kidnapped and reanimated. But you try to ignore your doubts. You realize that Master Igor has always been lonely. He never had any child to pass his knowledge on to. You are both orphans. Sometimes you feel connected to him.

But a week later, there's a furious pounding on the front door. When you open it, you're shocked. It's Eleanor, alive! A greasy old man has bound her with ropes and a gag.

"Tell your master we finally caught her," the man says.

You hope it's some kind of mistake, but Master Igor orders Eleanor to be imprisoned in the house. It appears that he gave orders for Eleanor to be murdered! She escaped, but now Igor's men have caught her again.



GO ON TO THE NEXT PAGE.

GO ON TO THE NEXT PAGE.

Eleanor's offer is tempting, if you can get anyone else to believe the story.

**WILL YOU . . .**

. . . help Eleanor escape?
TURN TO PAGE 53.

. . . lock her back in the room? With Eleanor out of the way, you'll get everything.
TURN TO PAGE 111.

"Someone please help me!" the resurrection man screams again, running from the monster.

You and Eleanor dash into the street.

"Stop!" you yell.

The monster pauses.

"What is it wearing?" you ask Eleanor. "It looks like . . ."

"A police uniform," she finishes.

The monster raises its eyes. They glow with inhuman intensity. *"Where is she?"* it roars.

"Someone's coming," Eleanor says.

"Catch that thing!" a man shouts. Six or seven people rush past you and Eleanor. They toss a net over the monster's head. The resurrection man tries to escape, but they capture him too.

At first you think it's the police, but your saviors are wearing servant uniforms. One of them approaches. "You're Eleanor, right? My master wants to speak to you . . . and your friend."

"Your master?"

"The Earl of Bridgeport."

COME IN, COME IN!
WHAT COULD AN EARL WANT WITH ME?
AND HOW DID HE KNOW ABOUT THE MONSTER?
ELEANOR! IT IS YOU. ARE YOU FAMISHED? TAKE SOME TEA.
YOU KNOW HIM?
I'VE NEVER SEEN HIM BEFORE!
YOU MUST BE WONDERING WHY I BROUGHT YOU HERE. THE TRUTH, MY DEAR, IS THAT I KNEW YOUR LATE FATHER.
MY FATHER? BUT...I GREW UP IN AN ORPHANAGE.
YOUR DEAR LATE FATHER ENTRUSTED YOUR CARE TO ME. BUT THEY SAID YOU HAD DIED, AND SO YOUR FATHER'S APPRENTICE INHERITED HIS MONEY AND HIS WORK.
HIS APPRENTICE?
YES, HIS APPRENTICE, ICHABOD IGOR.
MASTER IGOR! THEN THAT MEANS THAT ELEANOR'S FATHER IS...
DOCTOR FRANKENSTEIN!
DOCTOR FRANKENSTEIN!

Growing up in the orphanage, the nuns would tell you of the evil Doctor Frankenstein—the mad doctor who learned to harness the power of electricity to create monsters. Living corpses.

"The creature in the alley," you say. "That's one of Frankenstein's creations?"

The earl looks calmly at you. "No," he says. "That was the work of your Master Igor. You never suspected what he was doing?"

You did always wonder. But it seemed too impossible. Eleanor holds her head in her hands.

"Frankenstein," she whispers. "I grew up with that book . . . Why did no one tell me?"

TURN TO PAGE 72.

You and Eleanor stand side by side, shocked.

"Could it be that both of you have found each other?" asks Priscilla, the old maid. "The two lost children of Doctor Frankenstein?"

You never once suspected that you could have been in the same orphanage as Eleanor for a reason. And now to learn that she's your sister and you're both heirs to Doctor Frankenstein's fortune!

"But . . ." Eleanor says, "How can you know it's us?"

"That watch by your side, dear. And I suspect your friend has one as well."

You both take out the watches, inscribed with Doctor Frankenstein's initials: V.F.

"Here," Priscilla says. "I think you should have this." She hands you a stack of papers tied with twine. You read the title: *The Tale of My Life,* by Victor Frankenstein.

"This is what you have sought, am I right?"

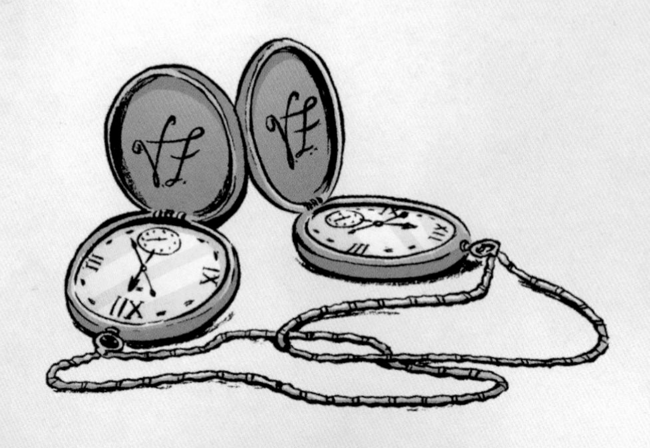




GO ON TO THE NEXT PAGE.

Finally, you've found Frankenstein's diary!

## WILL YOU . . .

. . . suggest burning it? Maybe you'll be safer with the past buried.
TURN TO PAGE 102.

. . . suggest turning it over to Crosdale? He may be a monster, but he hasn't betrayed you yet.
TURN TO PAGE 34.

You gulp. "I'll go first."

"Hurry!" Eleanor says. The secret door rattles like someone is trying to enter. You swing your leg over the edge of the windowsill and start to climb down. You take deep breaths and try not to look down. Before you know it, you're on the ground, Eleanor beside you.

"We have to go back to the earl's house," she says. "I *knew* there was something strange about him."

But when you and Eleanor finally arrive at the earl's house, you find everything in confusion.

"The prisoner has escaped!" one of the servants says.

"What happened?"

"Lightning struck. He seemed to glow . . . and then he broke out. I'd like to know what sort of man can bend solid iron."

You remember how the detective looked back in the graveyard. And poor Isabel wired up in Igor's lab. Is it possible . . .

Eleanor grips your elbow. "I think Detective Crosdale must be . . ."

You look at her in horror. "Reanimated!"



GO ON TO THE NEXT PAGE.

HE MUST HAVE BEEN IN A HURRY.
LOOK--A TRAIL OF TOBACCO. MAYBE HE HAS A HOLE IN HIS POCKET.

A FEW PEOPLE SAW HIM...

...AND THE CLUES LEAD YOU TO TWO DIFFERENT PLACES.
THAT COULD BE FROM A COPPER'S UNIFORM.

A DANGEROUS LOCAL PUB...
the BEAGLE

...OR SCOTLAND YARD ITSELF. WHERE HIS FELLOW OFFICERS PLANNED TO KILL HIM.

GO ON TO THE NEXT PAGE.

The clues lead to two places.

# WILL YOU CHOOSE . . .

. . . the dangerous pub?
TURN TO PAGE 87.

. . . Scotland Yard?
TURN TO PAGE 92.

You watch nervously as Officer Clive and that other man disappear. Eventually, Detective Crosdale returns. He looks distracted and upset.

"Um . . . sir?" you say. You tell him about Officer Clive and the strange man. "I think you might be in danger."

Detective Crosdale rubs his temples and starts to pace in front of you. "There's no time," he mutters. "Everything is moving too quickly."

"Sir? Can I help?"

Crosdale looks up at you. Suddenly, he smiles, as though he is seeing you for the first time. "The girl is missing," Crosdale says. "But yes, you might do very well. Follow me."

You don't understand what he means, but you trust him. He leads you down the same dark hallway where you last saw Clive.

"I want to show you something," Crosdale says. Your heart pounds with excitement. You can't believe that you get to share an investigation with your hero!

To your confusion, Crosdale pours an odd-smelling liquid on a cloth. "Here," he says. "Smell this."

You do. Almost immediately, your vision goes fuzzy. You see Crosdale's face. He looks . . . sad.

"I'm sorry," Crosdale says. "I don't have much choice."

GO ON TO THE NEXT PAGE.

You awake in darkness. A rough burlap bag scratches your skin. People are speaking above you. After a moment, you recognize the voices: Crosdale and Master Igor! You try to speak, but a gag is in your mouth.

"This one knows all your secrets, Igor," says Crosdale. "With the girl gone, the child is your only liability."

"Why, Crosdale?" says Master Igor. "You know what use I'd have for more human parts in my lab. I know how you hate me. How can I trust you?"

"Because you have Isabel," Crosdale says. His voice shakes, like he might cry. You wonder who Isabel is.

Igor barks a laugh. "You want your monster bride? And you will leave me alone forever?"

"You have my word," Crosdale says.

You try to move, but the burlap is tight around you. After a few moments, a woman enters the room. "Oh, Lance!" she cries. "Let's leave this foul place."

You realize, too late, that they're walking to the door. Frantically, you try to squirm out of Igor's grasp.

"You're all mine," Igor says and places his strong hands around your neck . . .

***THE END***

YOU FOLLOW IGOR ALL DAY.

BUT NOTHING HAPPENS...

...UNTIL EARL BRIDGEPORT FINALLY LEAVES, THAT IS.

IS SOMEONE THERE?

HOW ODD...

HE ALMOST CAUGHT US!

GO ON TO THE NEXT PAGE.

# WILL YOU . . .

. . . try to get into the tower from inside?
TURN TO PAGE 50.

. . . try to climb the tower from the outside?
TURN TO PAGE 75.

You see dark clouds roiling in the sky and hear the rumble of thunder. You don't want to be caught outside.

"I think I should be going now, sir. My Master Igor will be upset with me—"

Finally, Crosdale looks up from the gravestone. He stares at you with terror-filled eyes. "Igor? Ichabod Igor?"

"I'm his servant, yes," you say. "But what—"

Detective Crosdale grabs you by the shoulder. Lightning strikes. In the sudden light, his eyes look wild. "His horrible experiments . . . you must never go back!"

Crosdale wrenches himself away. For a moment, you think he might cry. Then a bolt of lightning strikes Crosdale himself, with a mighty crash. You scream. But instead of burning to a crisp, Crosdale seems to . . . glow. A moment later, he turns to you, all traces of humanity vanished from his eyes. The lightning has transformed him.

"No!" he screams. Then his fist slams into your jaw.

The next morning, a grumpy caretaker kicks you awake. "How'd you get in here? Out, before I call the coppers!"

You run out of the graveyard, shivering at the thought of Crosdale. You don't know *what* to call the detective, but you know it will never be "hero" again.

***THE END***

You watch as Crosdale brushes past you, but do nothing. You wonder if you see a "thank you" in his eyes, but you'll never be sure . . .

. . . because no one sees or hears from the famous detective Lance Crosdale ever again.

The police commissioner is disappointed, but he isn't angry. Perhaps he knows why you let Crosdale pass. He might have been a monster, but inside his monstrous body was the same detective you admired.

"Well," the commissioner says, when the police can discover no trace of Crosdale, "I can't very well send you two back to Ichabod Igor."

"What are we going to do?" you ask. "Our parents are dead."

The commissioner smiles. "I thought you might like to work here."

So you and Eleanor take work running errands and writing notes for the police. You're happy—the commissioner says that in a few years, you might train to be a detective. Then one day, two months after Crosdale's escape, you hear strange news.

"Master Igor is dead!" Eleanor tells you breathlessly that day. "Someone killed him and destroyed his experiments!"

THE HORN
Ichabod Igor, scientist, murdered
Police suspect "lightning killer"


They never do catch the killer. It's the one case you never try to solve.



***THE END***

I'LL... J-JUST GO TO SLEEP NOW, MASTER IGOR.
YOU GET AWAY FROM HIM AS SOON AS YOU CAN.
BUT SOMETHING ABOUT MASTER IGOR MAKES YOU TOO NERVOUS. SO THE NEXT MORNING, YOU TAKE WHAT YOU OWN AND GO TO THE MARKET.
WORK? DON'T HAVE ANY MESELF. BUT YOU MIGHT TRY ASKING TRAVERS, A BIT DOWN THE WAY. YOU'LL KNOW HIM BY THE DIRT UNDER HIS NAILS. LOTS OF WORK LIKE THAT, THESE DAYS.
the BEAGLE
WORK? I MIGHT, AT THAT, IF YOU DON'T MIND GETTING YOUR HANDS DIRTY. MIGHT YOU BE GAME FOR A BIT OF GRAVEYARD DIGGING?

"There is much tragedy in your past, my dear," the earl says. "You were your parents' only surviving child. They doted on you. And now that we have found each other, we need to find evidence that will defeat Igor."

"And how can we do that?"

He smiles. "I have a plan."

A servant opens the door and pokes his head inside. "Begging pardon, my lord. The prisoner is subdued in the cellar."

"Good," says the earl. "And you two should rest."

"What about the prisoner in the basement?" Eleanor whispers to you, as you walk through the rich hallways of the earl's home. "Should we try to speak to him?"



GO ON TO THE NEXT PAGE.

TWISTED JOURNEYS®

# WILL YOU . . .

. . . agree and sneak away to find the prisoner? You don't know how much you trust this earl.
TURN TO PAGE 100.

. . . say no? It's late, and you don't want the earl to catch you snooping.
TURN TO PAGE 12.

You scramble from behind the gurney and dash down the hall. You try to be quiet as you follow the two men out a back door. In the chill night air, the resurrection man lights his pipe. Neither seems to have noticed your presence, and you breathe a sigh of relief.

"We need to get rid of that *thing* once and for all," says Officer Clive.

The resurrection man blows a plume of smoke into Officer Clive's sallow face. "That *thing* is the most famous detective in Britain."

You choke back a gasp. They must be talking about Crosdale! You clench your fists in anger. These fiends actually plan to murder your hero! *And* steal his body? Why else would anyone plot with a resurrection man?

"I don't care if he is famous. Just do your job."

"And what about the body?" asks the resurrection man.

"Ichabod Igor will pay well, I'm sure," says Officer Clive.

Master Igor! But it only makes sense that he would be involved in such dirty business.

TURN TO PAGE 78.

GO ON TO THE NEXT PAGE.

Eleanor puts her hand to her mouth and gasps.

You don't even know what to say. The monsters were bad enough, but this room terrifies you.

"I knew Igor was terrible . . ." you say.

Eleanor takes a few steps closer to the pulsing brain. Suddenly she shrieks.

"What is it?"

"Something . . . the brain is moving something."

Sure enough, you can see that one of the wires leading from the brain is attached to some sort of mechanical device. At the end of its long arm is a pen.

"It's . . . writing something," you say.

You and Eleanor watch silently as the words form on the page.

`My daughter, is that you?`

"F-frankenstein?" she says. "Father?"

You can't believe it. Master Igor has captured Frankenstein's brain!

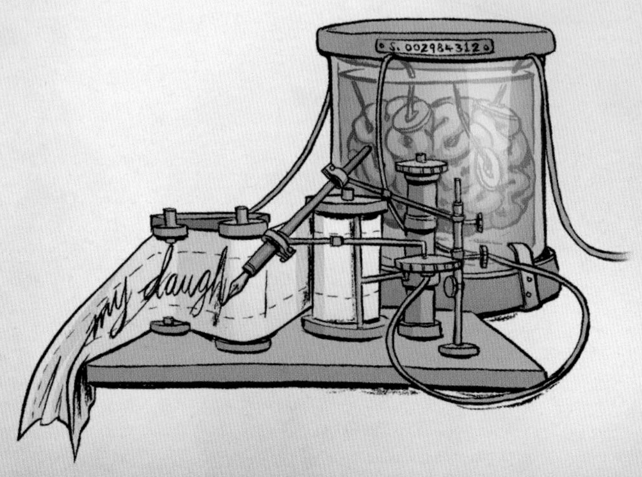




TURN TO PAGE 26.

IN THE NAME OF HER MAJESTY THE QUEEN, WE HEREBY ARREST YOU!
THE WORK YOU DO WITH OFFICER BUSHWICK ISN'T GLAMOROUS.

OFTEN YOU CAN'T EVEN ARREST THE ONES WHO BUY THE STOLEN CADAVERS.

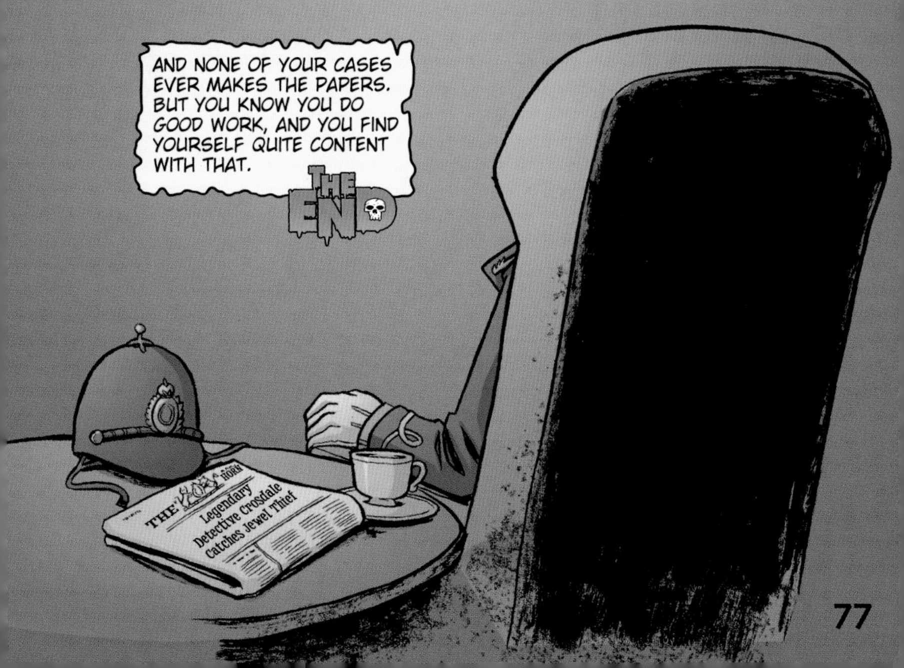
AND NONE OF YOUR CASES EVER MAKES THE PAPERS. BUT YOU KNOW YOU DO GOOD WORK, AND YOU FIND YOURSELF QUITE CONTENT WITH THAT.
THE END
Legendary Detective Crosdale Catches Jewel Thief

"Wait!" says Officer Clive, "I hear that sound again."

Uh-oh. You run back through the hallway. They chase after you.

"Come back here!" Officer Clive shouts.

You run so fast that you don't notice the figure at the end of the hallway.

"Whoa, hold on there, child," says the man, after you careen into his stomach. "What's the rush?"

"I . . . there's a resurrection man and . . ."

The man peers at you more closely. "Wait, I say, aren't you that one who was helping Detective Crosdale?"

You realize who you're speaking to: it's the police commissioner! He looked unfriendly earlier, but now you wonder if you misjudged him.

Officer Clive has caught up. "Sir," he says, "I think that little rat was eavesdropping."

"Were you?" asks the commissioner. "And why would you do that?"

The police commissioner looks friendly now, but he seemed to be arguing with Detective Crosdale earlier. Who's to say that he isn't part of Officer Clive's plot to kill your hero?



GO ON TO THE NEXT PAGE.

WILL YOU . . .

. . . decide to trust the commissioner and tell him what you heard?
TURN TO PAGE 96.

. . . lie and find Crosdale immediately? He has to be warned!
TURN TO PAGE 16.

"No way!" you tell Eleanor. "How can we trust Igor will keep his part of the bargain, anyway. It's better to get the inheritance."

"Well?" Igor says. "Give me a good reason why I shouldn't kill the lot of you."

"The whole world is going to know," you say. "We've given Frankenstein's diary to a reporter."

Igor goes pale. "You found it? Oh, that blasted Crosdale!"

From the chair, Crosdale groans. "Run," he says weakly. "Run, children."

Igor laughs and opens a door behind him. "Come out, darling."

It's another monster! Only this one acts nothing like Crosdale. It glows and growls like an animal.

"Get them!" Igor says.

You barely take a step before you feel the thing's hand on your back.

"The world will learn what a monster you are, Igor," you say. But the last thing you hear is only a harsh crunch.

*THE END*

He killed our first child, you see. Though we did not know it at the time.
FAREWELL, OUR BELOVED CHILD

He longed for my inheritance. Which he would never get, with you **alive**.

OUR LADY OF MERCY ORPHANAGE
So the handmaid hid you as best she could.

MASTER IGOR HAS AGREED TO TAKE ON YOU AND YOUR FRIEND, DEAR. SAY "THANK YOU."
THANK YOU.
But one day, he found you.

Do you still have the watch I left you, my dear?
BUT... THAT'S JUST LIKE MY OWN...

You've never been happier to see Master Igor's house. Now all his evil will be stopped forever.

"My father . . ." Eleanor says, as you watch the police enter the house. "He should never have made that monster."

"And Igor should never have stolen your inheritance," you say.

Together, you enter the house. There are officers everywhere. One officer has Master Igor, still in his nightdress and cap.

"You can't do this!" Master Igor shouts. "I've done nothing wrong!"

Detective Crosdale loosens his collar and stands in front of Master Igor. You gasp. Now you can clearly see the stitches of his reanimated body.

"You've done a great deal wrong, Igor."

Master Igor turns pale as a ghost. "You . . . you told them?"

"And now there's nothing you can threaten me with."

Master Igor is shipped to the faraway prison colony of Australia with other criminals. And after the police find Doctor Frankenstein's will, Eleanor becomes rich. As for you, the commissioner is impressed with your detection skills. He makes you the youngest detective on the force. Your dream has finally come true!

**THE END**

# WILL YOU . . .

. . . deny the truth when Charlie prints it in the paper? At least that way you'll save Crosdale's life.
TURN TO PAGE 98.

. . . refuse to go along with Eleanor's plan. You just found out you're heir to a fortune—how can you give that up now?
TURN TO PAGE 80.

THE COMMISSIONER TOLD YOU CLIVE WOULD BE GONE FOR A FEW HOURS.
HOPEFULLY YOU CAN FIND WHAT YOU'RE LOOKING FOR IN HIS BELONGINGS.

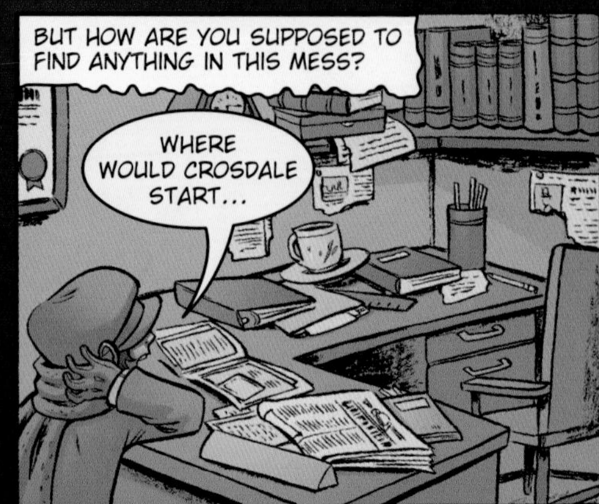

BUT HOW ARE YOU SUPPOSED TO FIND ANYTHING IN THIS MESS?
WHERE WOULD CROSDALE START...

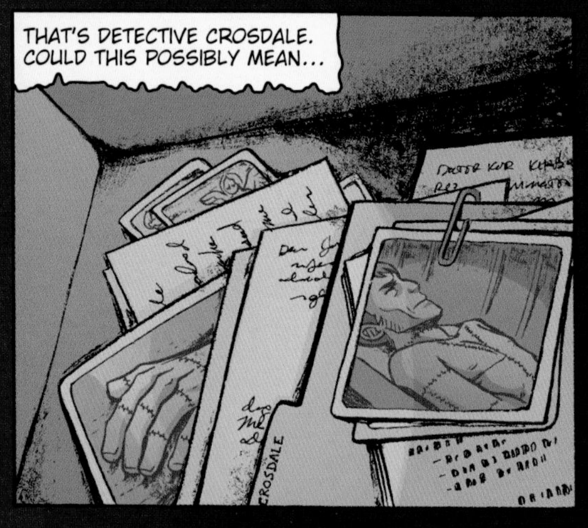

THAT'S DETECTIVE CROSDALE. COULD THIS POSSIBLY MEAN...
CROSDALE

SO NOW YOU KNOW THE TRUTH.

TURN TO PAGE 10.

"Master Igor wouldn't hide something so important in his study," you say. "Let's try the graveyard."

Eleanor agrees, and so the two of you slip out of the house, unnoticed. The night isn't cold, but Eleanor still shivers when you reach the imposing gates of Kensal Green.

"Are you all right?" you ask.

She nods. You remember that just a few days ago, men kidnapped her and brought her here. You're sure she's scared, but she'll never admit it.

You climb over the gate. Eleanor looks around nervously, but tonight you're alone in the graveyard.

"Let's start with Frankenstein's grave," you say.

Eleanor squares her shoulders. "This way," she says. "Master Igor brought me here once, when I first came from the orphanage."

Frankenstein's grave is a marble tomb, like a little stone house. The lock on the front gate is rusted. You break it easily.

Inside, there is an urn with an inscription: "For my beloved children."

GO ON TO THE NEXT PAGE.

Eleanor frowns and lifts the urn. "For my beloved children?" she reads, again. "But what could he mean?"

"Maybe you have a sister or a brother?" you say. "Wait, look, there's something in the wall . . ."

Behind the urn, there's a small drawer in the wall. Carefully, Eleanor pulls it open. The clouds of disturbed dust make you cough.

Eleanor lights a long match. In the light, you can clearly see the outline in the dust where a rectangular object once lay.

"There was a book here," she says. "But someone must have stolen it."

You can't hide your disappointment. It's almost dawn. You return to Bridgeport empty-handed.

He's not happy.

"I should have known better than to trust you to find this," he says, with a strange smile. "But you may stay on as my servants, if you wish."

And so you and Eleanor live your lives as servants in the earl's house. It's not a bad life, but some nights you remember how much more you could have had.

*THE END*

DETECTIVE CROSDALE CAME HERE? I'M NOT SO SURE ABOUT THIS.
WAIT, THOSE MEN LOOK FAMILIAR.
YOU RECOGNIZE THEM TOO. YOUR STOMACH SINKS.
WELL, LOOK AT THAT.
THE BIRDIE FLEW STRAIGHT HOME. AND THE OTHER ONE IGOR WANTED TOO!
ELEANOR, RUN!
OOF! COME BACK HERE, KID!
THEY'RE TOO STRONG FOR YOU...
CRACK
HE'S THE LAST THING YOU SEE BEFORE YOU PASS OUT...

"Of course I want your help!" you say. "I've read your book. I want to be a detective more than anything."

Crosdale takes a puff on his pipe and looks away. "It . . . can be a dangerous life."

"I don't care," you say. "I need to find Eleanor."

Crosdale smiles and pockets his pipe. "Then let's look for clues, shall we?"

The two coppers are gone when you go back inside.

"This might help us," Crosdale says, taking a brown sack from the corner.

"What's that?" you ask.

"Your friend Eleanor's belongings."

He opens it, and what you find surprises you: a tarnished pocket watch, much like the one you've also had all your life. And an old, musty book.

"Curious," says Crosdale. "I remember reading this in my youth."

You look at the title: *The Modern Prometheus,* by Mary Shelley. "Is that the one about the doctor who . . ."

"Yes," Crosdale says, with a quirk of his eyebrows. "Doctor Frankenstein."

GO ON TO THE NEXT PAGE.

GO ON TO THE NEXT PAGE.

You don't trust that Officer Clive at all, and they seemed to know something about Eleanor.

# WILL YOU . . .

. . . wait here for Detective Crosdale?
TURN TO PAGE 65.

. . . chase after them?
TURN TO PAGE 74.

"Fetch a doctor," you tell Eleanor. You press your hand to the bloody wound in Crosdale's side. He groans.

"But he's already reanimated. How can a normal doctor help him?"

You realize she's right. "But that means . . ."

"We have to ask Master Igor for help."

From the floor, the resurrection man mumbles. And there's a commotion in the bar just outside.

"Hurry!" you say.

Eleanor puts her shoulder under Crosdale's other arm, and together you drag him to the back door that leads to an alley. It's open from Charlie's escape.

"Do you think Igor will help us?" you ask Eleanor.

She leans down and picks up a few of the papers from Frankenstein's diary that fell in the alleyway. "Maybe if we offer him something he wants," she says.

TURN TO PAGE 30.

The police commissioner is there when you enter Scotland Yard. "You want Detective Crosdale? Follow me."

"Here you go," says the commissioner, opening a door. "Just filing reports."

You and Eleanor gasp. Detective Crosdale is sitting behind a desk. He looks completely normal.

"Now what's this?" asks the commissioner, frowning.

"I think we should tell him," Eleanor whispers. "Horrible things are happening at Master Igor's. That woman . . . *someone* needs to know!"

You tell the commissioner almost everything. As you speak, Crosdale stands up and takes a few steps forward.

"And there's one more thing," you say with a gulp. "D-detective Crosdale . . ."

"No!" says the detective.

"He's one of them," Eleanor says. "A monster."

Crosdale starts to run for the door.

"Stop him!" the commissioner shouts.

GO ON TO THE NEXT PAGE

You're the closest to the door.

# WILL YOU . . .

. . . ignore the commissioner and let Crosdale escape? He has always been your hero.
TURN TO PAGE 70.

. . . stick out your foot and trip the escaping detective?
TURN TO PAGE 104.

You take one last look at Detective Crosdale, bleeding on the floor, before you sprint after the reporter. You can help Crosdale later. Pages of the diary flutter behind Charlie, forming a trail. Your breath comes short, but you push yourself harder.

"Come back!" you shout.

You don't realize where Charlie's headed until it's too late. He's taken you to a part of the city you don't know at all. You follow him into an alley. Though you hear him, you can't see him anywhere. You look around: you're hopelessly lost!

You wander around until morning, when you find a friendly copper to direct you back home. But it's too late. Charlie has printed the story in the paper—along with another headline:

"Lance Crosdale dies of gunshot wound in the night."

**THE END**

THERE SHE IS.
SLIPPERY, AIN'T SHE?
ELEANOR!
STOP!
YOU GONNA DO SOMETHIN' ABOUT IT, KID?
B-BEHIND YOU...
YOU HEAR AN UNEARTHLY GROAN AND HEAVY FOOTSTEPS.
LET'S GO!
AARGH!
SIZZLE
YEARS LATER, YOU'LL TELL THE STORY OF THE MONSTER THAT SAVED YOUR LIFE. TOO BAD NO ONE EVER BELIEVES YOU.
THE

"I'll tell you," you say, "but in private."

The police commissioner waves Clive away and takes you to his office.

"Now, what is this business?" he says once you are alone.

You tell him everything that you overheard—how Clive and resurrection men and other officers are plotting to murder Detective Crosdale.

The police commissioner looks grave as you tell your story. "This is serious business, indeed. But I need more evidence before I can accuse my own men. I need someone to investigate for me. Someone who won't raise suspicion. Will you help me?"

"Of course!" you say.

"Good," says the commissioner. "I'll leave it up to you which officer you investigate first. You could start with Officer Clive. But I have my suspicions of Officer Bushwick, as well."

"Officer Bushwick?" you ask. Wasn't he the kind man who brought you there from your employer's house?

"Choose wisely. If it's as you say, Detective Crosdale's life is in danger."

GO ON TO THE NEXT PAGE.

# WILL YOU . . .

. . . investigate Officer Bushwick? You don't know him, but if the commissioner is suspicious, he must have a good reason.
TURN TO PAGE 47.

. . . investigate Officer Clive? After all, you *heard* him plotting to kill Crosdale.
TURN TO PAGE 84.

"We've found Frankenstein's memoirs," you say. "And we've given them to a reporter. If you agree to save Crosdale, we'll deny whatever he says."

Igor narrows his eyes. "How can I trust you?"

Eleanor swallows. "We'll burn these pages of the memoir. Without them, there isn't any evidence that we're his children."

"You'll renounce the inheritance?"

You look at Crosdale, your hero, bleeding slowly onto the floor. "Yes," you say. "We will."

Igor takes Crosdale to the lab. You watch in horror and fascination as he uses his scientific tools to give Crosdale new organs and skin. Then he hooks Crosdale to the wires hanging from the ceiling.

"Stand back!" Igor says. He pulls a lever on the wall. Electrical light courses through the wires and into Crosdale's body.

"I . . . where am I?" the detective says weakly. Then he groans. "Oh no . . . have you brought me back again, Igor?"

You and Eleanor look at each other. You've made your decision. You can only hope that it was the right one.



**THE END**

CRASH
UGH...
UGH...
AWAKE,
ARE WE?
YOUR BODY FEELS SO...
STRANGE. LIKE IT ISN'T
YOUR OWN ANYMORE.
WHAT'S
HAPPENING?
NOOOO!
BUT IT'S TRUE. MASTER
IGOR AND THE EARL
HAVE TURNED YOU INTO...
A MONSTER.
THE END

You check to see if the hallways are clear and then meet Eleanor at the top of the servants' staircase.

"The dungeon is this way," Eleanor says. "I overheard the servants."

There is a long, dark hallway that ends in a door with long metal bars.

"Who's there?" says the thing behind the door. His voice is raspy, like sandpaper. Yet you can't help but think it's familiar. "I told you, Bridgeport," he says, "there's nothing you can get from me."

With a sense of horror, you look closer. Your hero, Detective Crosdale, is one of Master Igor's graveyard monsters?

"It's you," he says. "Please, you must help me!" He hands you a rumpled piece of paper. "Someone must find Frankenstein's diary. Won't you please follow the clues for me?"

"Yes!" Eleanor says, and you know she wants to know what her father might have written.

The clues lead to an alley behind a dingy tavern. But someone has beaten you there!

"Those urchins are stealing the papers!" Eleanor says.

GO ON TO THE NEXT PAGE.

If you hurry you might be able to catch them.

# WILL YOU . . .

. . . alert the nearby police officer who has just staggered out of the pub?

TURN TO PAGE 25.

. . . chase after them?

TURN TO PAGE 39.

"We should burn this, Eleanor," you say. "Maybe Igor will leave us alone if we just stop pursuing this."

"I think you speak wisely," Priscilla says.

Eleanor stands up, but Charlie, the urchin, suddenly runs in front of her.

"Wait!" he says. "Don't you at least want to read what's in the book? Your father went through a lot of trouble to leave that for you."

"I don't know how much more I can bear to learn about our father," Eleanor says.

But together, you and your newfound sister read through Frankenstein's papers. Then you toss them in the fire.

The next morning, you and Eleanor are shocked to discover that the *Daily Horn* has a front-page story all about Doctor Frankenstein, his two long-lost children, and Master Igor. The writer? Charlie Anders.

"That urchin boy!" Eleanor says. "He wasn't as young as we thought."

You and Eleanor hide and leave the city that night. Now that he's been ruined, Master Igor will stop at nothing to hurt you both. But as you walk down the road away from London, you look forward to a new beginning.

**THE END**

KENSAL GREEN. PERHAPS ELEANOR WOULD HAVE RESTED IN PEACE HERE, IF ONLY HER BODY HADN'T BEEN STOLEN.
WAIT, WHAT'S THAT?
HOW DARE THEY?
WAIT, NO! YOU MUSTN'T! IT...ISN'T SAFE.
BUT THEY'RE STEALING THOSE BODIES!
THERE'S NOTHING WE CAN DO...
BELIEVE ME. I KNOW MORE THAN YOU COULD IMAGINE ABOUT THOSE FIENDS...
WHAT'S WRONG WITH CROSDALE? HE'S A COPPER--WHY CAN'T HE JUST ARREST THE RESURRECTION MEN?

AHH!
SO IGOR REANIMATED YOU? AND YOUR FIANCÉE? WHEN DID THIS HAPPEN, LANCE?
ALMOST A YEAR AGO NOW. HE KNEW OF MY INVESTIGATION INTO HIS PAST WITH FRANKENSTEIN. SO HE KILLED ME.

ARGH!
"BUT WHY WOULD IGOR BRING YOU BACK TO LIFE?"
WHAT... HOW...
MY FINEST CREATION.
I HAVE GIVEN YOU BACK YOUR LIFE, DETECTIVE. AND NOW YOU WILL NEVER BE ABLE TO HARM ME. THE MOMENT YOU TELL THE WORLD MY SECRET, I'LL TELL THEM YOURS.

I TRIED TO CONTINUE MY WORK...
BUT THEN HE TOOK MY ISABEL.

Everyone is silent once Crosdale finishes his story. You feel terrible for ever doubting him.

"Why didn't you just tell me, Lance?" the commissioner asks.

"I'm a monster! The other officers found out and were planning to kill me because of what I am. I didn't know who to trust."

"Well," says the commissioner. "You can trust me now. I believe we have work to do."

It turns out the commissioner has known of Master Igor's crimes for many months. But now, with everyone's stories, he can finally put a stop to Igor. He rouses every detective and officer in Scotland Yard.

"We're arresting Ichabod Igor," he tells them.

"And not that . . . monster?" You recognize the voice: Officer Clive. The one who was plotting to kill Crosdale.

"I don't think that Crosdale is the monster here," the commissioner says. "We're going to stop Igor from using Frankenstein's reanimation machine on anyone else."

TURN TO PAGE 82.

"Can I help?" you ask.

Crosdale smiles at you. "We can still investigate, now, can't we?" he says.

You're relieved when he leads you closer to the resurrection men. "Something is strange here," Crosdale says. He points to a large sack, resting beside the grave. Whatever is inside . . . is moving.

"Ho there!" says Detective Crosdale. "What are you doing?"

One of the resurrection men spits into the dirt. "Faugh. Same as you, I imagine. What else to do in a boneyard past midnight, eh?"

"It's not often one of you brings in a live body, though." Crosdale gestures to the squirming bundle. The resurrection men look uncomfortable. You hear a sudden crash of thunder. There's a storm coming.

Crosdale looks at you in panic. You don't understand why until it's too late. Lightning streaks into the graveyard and strikes him.

"Stay back!" He stumbles away before you can stop him. The resurrection men run also. Through the pouring rain, you look back down and see the resurrection men have left the squirming sack.



GO ON TO THE NEXT PAGE.

ELEANOR!!

YOU WANTED TO FIND HER, BUT YOU DIDN'T DARE HOPE SHE'D BE ALIVE.

I DON'T KNOW WHAT YOU'RE DOING HERE, BUT YOU HAVE TO LEAVE.
I BARELY ESCAPED THOSE MEN ALIVE. YOU'RE NOT SAFE.

LEAVE. I NEED TO DO THIS, BUT I DON'T WANT YOUR HELP.
BUT... AREN'T WE FRIENDS, ELEANOR?
THAT'S WHY I WANT TO KEEP YOU SAFE.

You can't just let Eleanor go out there by herself! But she seems pretty determined.

## WILL YOU . . .

. . . make her go back home with you, even if you have to drag her?
TURN TO PAGE 22.

. . . pretend to let her go and follow her?
TURN TO PAGE 48.

"We'll just take the papers, thanks," you say. Eleanor empties her pockets of all her money, and the urchin hands over the papers.

"Fine. But watch out. It gets dangerous around here."

You and Eleanor leave the alley. She pauses to look at the papers Crosdale asked you to find. They are actually photographs, like the ones in the paper each morning.

"How strange!" Eleanor says. You want to look more closely, but suddenly you hear footsteps.

"Over here!" someone whispers. The urchins from before? But no, there are too many of them.

"Let's run," Eleanor says.

You make it as far as the river, while your pursuers quickly catch up. When you have nowhere left to run, you turn around. It's a street gang. These kids are older. They look mean.

"What have we here?" says the oldest. He grins.

Someone hits you on the head, and you pass out. When you wake up, you and Eleanor are alone in an alley. They've taken some of your clothes and all of your money.

The urchin girl who first stole the photographs finds you. "You could beg with us," she offers . . .

THE END

Eleanor stares.

"You're right," she says. "But why would we have the same watch?"

Frankenstein's metallic pen trembles.

You were at the same orphanage. Could Priscilla have saved two children?

"Eleanor," you say, "could you be my sister?"

She gasps. "I must be!"

Igor will try to kill you both if he knows.

You try to wrap your mind around this. Frankenstein is your father! Eleanor is your sister!

"Father, how can we stop him?" she asks.

Don't trust Bridgeport, Frankenstein writes. Go to the police. That Detective Crosdale knows some of this. He has tried to stop Igor for years. Show him the watches.

So you climb back down the tower. At Scotland Yard, the commissioner is surprised, but eventually he believes you. The commissioner orders Master Igor arrested, and the officers find evidence of his plot to kill you both for the inheritance. Soon you both are rich. You live together in a great house, filled with the love of your newly discovered family.

*THE END*